THIS BOOK BELONGS TO

....

KALLIE GEORGE

SPARK

ILLUSTRATED BY

GENEVIÈVE CÔTÉ

SIMPLY READ BOOKS

For my dad, Tiffany and Luke—brilliant sparks in my life. – K.G.

For my friend Ronald, a.k.a. Ronnie Le Grand,
spectacular fire-breather. – G.C.

Published in 2013 by Simply Read Books
www.simplyreadbooks.com
Text © 2013 Kallie George
Illustrations © 2013 Geneviève Côté

Library and Archives Canada Cataloguing in Publication
George, K. (Kallie), 1983–
Spark / written by Kallie George ;
illustrated by Geneviève Côté.

ISBN 978-1-927018-24-8

I. Côté, Geneviève, 1964– II. Title.

PS8563.E6257S63 2013   JC813´.6   C2013-900910-8

We gratefully acknowledge for their financial support of our
publishing program the Canada Council for the Arts, the BC
Arts Council, and the Government of Canada through the
Canada Book Fund (CBF).

Manufactured in Malaysia.

Book design by Naomi MacDougall.

10 9 8 7 6 5 4 3 2 1

CONTENTS

Spark Gets His Flame

One day a tiny dragon
was born.

"What a pointy tail,"
said Mama.

"What a big snout,"
said Papa.

"And look!" added Mama.
"He is making sparks.
Let's name him Spark."

Spark grew fast.

First he grew a fang.
Then another.

Then he flew.

And then . . . BURP!
Out came a flame.

"Good job, Spark!"
said Mama.

"You are getting so big,"
said Papa. "But be
careful. Fire burns."

Spark tried to be careful.
It was hard.

ACHOO!
He set his hankie on fire.

COUGH! COUGH!
He set some leaves on fire.

Mama got a book:
How to Tame Flames.

Mama and Papa both read it.

LESSON 1:
Toast Marshmallows

Mama gave Spark a big bag.
It was full of marshmallows.

"Toast one at a time,"
she said. "Be careful.
Take a deep breath.
Blow out gently."

"I can do it!" said Spark.

He sat down. He put a
marshmallow on a stick.
He breathed in.
He breathed out.

WHOOSH!

Out came a big flame.

The marshmallow
caught fire.

CRACKLE. CRACKLE.

It burned to a crisp.

Spark tried again.

CRACKLE. CRACKLE.

Spark tried again and again.

Soon there was a huge pile
of burnt marshmallows.

Mama came over. She shook
her head. "Stop. This is not
working. We have to try
something else."

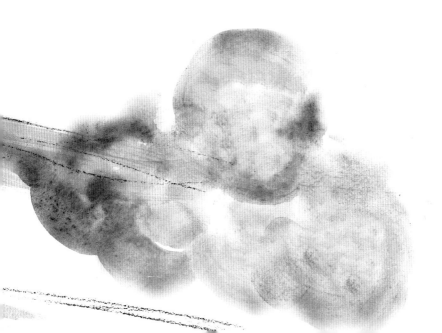

LESSON 2:
Dry the Dishes

"Go help Papa dry the dishes," said Mama. "Be careful. Take a deep breath. Blow out gently."

"I can do it!" said Spark.

Spark went into the kitchen.

The clean dishes were
piled in the sink.

He stood by them.

He breathed in.
He breathed out.

WHOOSH!

Out came a big flame.

The dishes heated up.

They glowed and then...

CRACK! CRACK!

Two dishes broke.

"Stop!" said Papa. "This is not working. We must try something else."

LESSON 3:
Try While You Sleep

It was bedtime.

Mama said, "Dream about taking a little breath. Dream about blowing out very gently. Dream about little flames."

"I can do it!" said Spark.

Spark closed his eyes.
He hugged his pillow.
Soon he was asleep.

He dreamed of breathing
in. He dreamed of breathing
out. He started to snore.

WHOOSH!

Out came a real flame.

POOF!
A cloud of smoke filled
his room.

Spark woke up.
"Mama! Papa!"

They rushed in.

"Don't worry," said Mama.
"Your bed is fireproof. Your
pillow is fireproof, too."

"But this is not working,"
said Papa. "You are too little
to control your flame.
Just wait. It will be easier
when you are older."

"Okay," said Spark.

He hoped Papa was right.

The Birthday Candles

Spark waited and waited.

Weeks went by.
Then months.
Soon it was his birthday.

Mama and Papa invited all
his friends to a party.

They had a picnic in
the woods.

Mama brought treats.

An apple for the
little unicorn.

A fish for the little griffin.

A worm for the little
phoenix.

A bowl of cold, lumpy
porridge for the little troll.

And a hot pepper for Spark.

The party was so much fun!

Spark was very careful.
He didn't sneeze fire.
He didn't cough fire.
He didn't even laugh fire.

"Time for the cake!"
said Mama.

"Let Spark light the candles!"
said his friends.

Mama and Papa nodded
at Spark. "You are older,"
said Papa.

"You can do it," said his friends.

Finally Spark said, "Okay. I will try."

Mama put the cake in front of Spark.

Spark closed his eyes.

He breathed in.

He breathed out VERY gently.

PIFF. PIFF.

Spark opened his eyes.
The candles were lit. Not
one bit of icing was melted.

"YAY!" yelled his friends.

"YAY!" yelled Spark.
"I did it!"

Everyone sang
"Happy Birthday."

"Time to put out the
candles," said Mama
and Papa.

Spark shook his head.

He didn't want to.

He was so proud of
lighting them.

THE END